NO LONGER PROPERTY OF
SEATTLE PUBLIC LIBRARY

D0564445

For my parents—
who taught me to dream, to always try,
and to never give up

Henry Holt and Company, *Publishers since 1866*
Henry Holt® is a registered trademark of Macmillan Publishing Group, LLC
175 Fifth Avenue, New York, New York 10010 • mackids.com

Copyright © 2019 by Jonathan D. Voss
All rights reserved.

Library of Congress Cataloging-in-Publication Data
Names: Voss, Jonathan D., author
Title: Imagine that : a Hoot & Olive story / Jonathan D. Voss.
Description: First edition. | New York : Henry Holt and Company, 2019. |
Summary: On a rainy day, perfect for a pretend adventure, Hoot finds that
his imagination is lost and Olive must find a way to restore it.
Identifiers: LCCN 2018039224 | ISBN 9781250314550 (hardcover)
Subjects: | CYAC: Imagination—Fiction. | Owls—Fiction.
Classification: LCC PZ7.1.V683 Im 2019 | DDC [E] —dc23
LC record available at https://lccn.loc.gov/2018039224

Our books may be purchased in bulk for promotional, educational, or business use.
Please contact your local bookseller or the Macmillan Corporate and Premium Sales Department
at (800) 221-7945 ext. 5442 or by email at MacmillanSpecialMarkets@macmillan.com.

First edition, 2019 / Designed by Patrick Collins
The artist used watercolor with pen and ink on Arches Hot Press Watercolor Board and
added color digitally to create the illustrations for this book.
Printed in China by RR Donnelley Asia Printing Solutions Ltd.,
Dongguan City, Guangdong Province

1 3 5 7 9 10 8 6 4 2

A Hoot & Olive Story

Imagine That

Jonathan D. Voss

Henry Holt and Company
New York

Olive had a great big imagination, which was only just a smidge smaller than her huge heart. Her best friend, Hoot, had a heart that was equally big. His imagination, however . . . Well, one rainy day, Hoot discovered something unexpected.

Olive tugged on Hoot's wing. "Let's go on a pretend adventure," she said. "Rainy days are perfect for that."

Hoot agreed. But in the very moment he
tried to imagine something magnificent,
he imagined nothing at all.

"I lost it," said Hoot.
"Lost what?" asked Olive.

"My imagination," he replied. "And
I can't remember where I had it last."
Then he got a more upsetting idea:
"Or maybe my imaginator is broken."

"I don't think it works like that," said Olive.
"But if it is broken, we should try to fix it."
"How?" said Hoot.
Olive was puzzled. "Actually, I don't know. You
just pretend like something is, even though it
really isn't."

Just then, the rain began to beat harder against the window.
"I know!" she said. "What if . . . the water gets higher than
just a little and the puddles grow really big?"
Suddenly, Olive felt the house lurch.

"Hoot!" cried Olive. "Do you feel that?
We're floating away!"

But Hoot felt nothing. "It's only a puddle," he said,
looking out the window.

Olive sighed. "A puddle isn't a very good adventure."

Then she got another idea.

"It looks like an antenna," said Hoot.

"Because it is," said Olive. "Your head must be all scrambly. That's why your imagination isn't working."

"How clever," said Hoot. "A head unscrambler."

Olive led Hoot into a room full of shadows.

She gasped. "Do you see that?" she said. "In the corner!"

"See what?" asked Hoot.

"The G-I-A-N-T," Olive whispered.

But Hoot saw nothing. "Maybe I blinked," he said.

"Or maybe it's worse than I thought," replied Olive.

So Olive tried earmuffs.

"For your leaky ears," she said.
"How elsc could your imagination
be escaping?"

"I guess that's why they tickle sometimes,"
said Hoot, following Olive to the cellar.

They stepped into the dark.
Something fluttered. Olive froze.

"Do you hear that?" she whispered.

"Fairies!"

But Hoot heard nothing.

"These ear mufflers might keep my insides from coming outside," he said, "but I can't hear anything with them on."

So Olive tried
something sleepy,

then something
upside down,

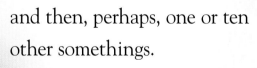

and then, perhaps, one or ten
other somethings.

But nothing worked.

"Maybe I can't be fixed," said
Hoot.

"Or maybe you're not really
trying," said Olive.

It was quiet for a long while.

Finally, in a small voice, Hoot spoke. "Why is it, when my imagination is the thing that's broken, it's my heart that hurts the most?"

"That's it!" shouted Olive. She had forgotten the most important part. "You have to imagine with this," she said, placing her hand over Hoot's heart.

"Should I try again?" asked Hoot.

"You should always try again," said Olive.

Hoot closed his eyes . . .

"I see something!" said Hoot. "But it's so small."

"That's how everything starts," replied Olive. "If you want it to grow, you have to love it."

So Hoot imagined again with his whole huge heart.

"You did it!" shouted Olive.
"Of course I did," said Hoot.

But that was only the beginning.

When the clouds broke and the world sparkled in the sun, Hoot and Olive's imaginations spilled onto everything. They sailed to far-off places and saw magnificent things. They built castles and tamed dragons. They were heroes and kings.

That day, they played till their
laughs finally turned to tired giggles.
"Thank you," said Hoot.
"For what?" asked Olive.
"For showing me the most
important part."
Olive smiled.

"What should we imagine tomorrow?" asked Hoot.

"We could be pirates," said Olive, "searching for treasure."

"That's an extra-good idea," said Hoot. "Do you think we could also imagine being friends forever?"

And they did. They imagined it all and so much more . . .

Both of them. Together.